PARIS

AND

PEANUTS

Teaching Children Through Animals
How to get Organized

Connie Pitts

ISBN 979-8-88644-933-4 (Paperback)
ISBN 979-8-88644-934-1 (Digital)

Covenant Books
11661 Hwy 707
Murrells Inlet, SC 29576
www.covenantbooks.com

To my beloved husband who loved our dogs unconditionally: The highlight of his day was to hold each one and have a conversation with them before he went to bed.

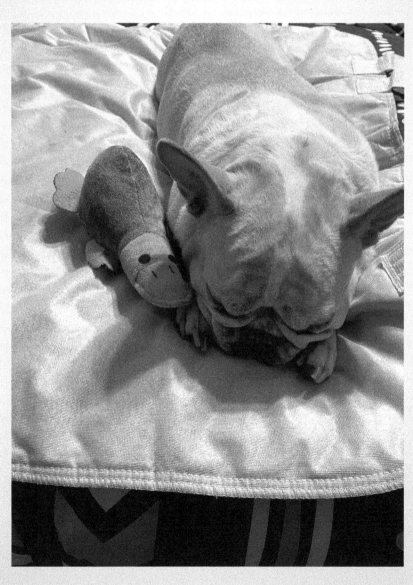

Paris is my French bulldog. She is so special—I want to introduce her to you.

She is my laughter, my companion, my follower, my understander, my everything.

She is *almost* perfect.

Paris, we need to talk. Are you listening?

"Uh–huh."

I need your help. You take Peanuts with you wherever you go.

"Uh–huh."

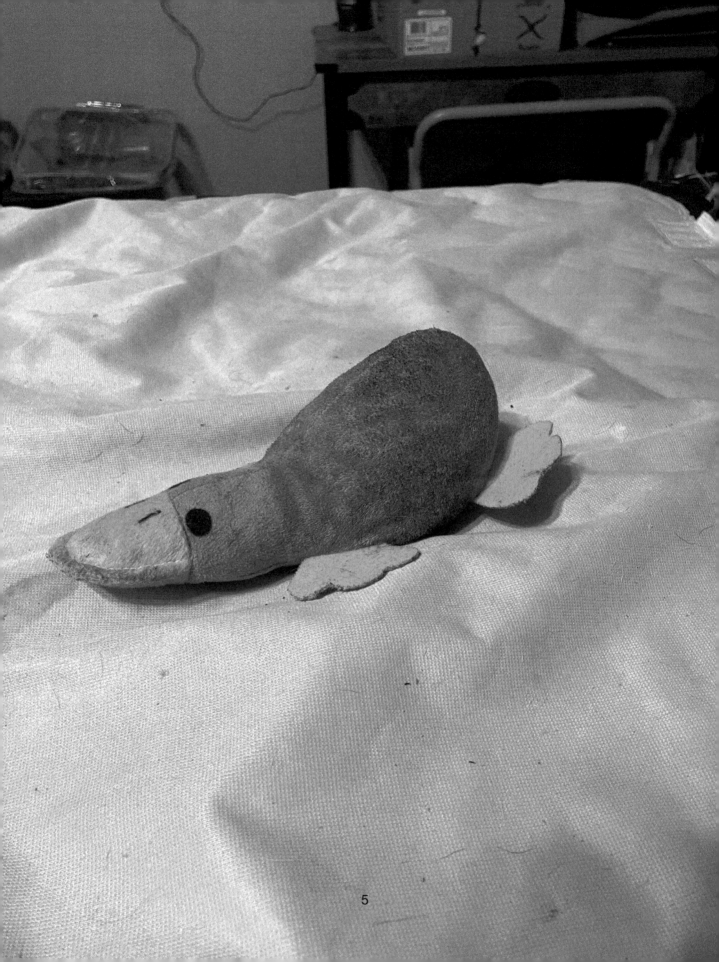

She is your baby. You can keep her forever.

"Uh–huh."

But you do need to get organized.

"What's orga–nized?"

For you, it means—

Putting Peanuts in a special place when you take her from room to room.

Sometimes I stumble over her. I know you don't want me to fall.

If I step on her, I could even hurt her.

You take her to every room in the house, and then you can't remember where you left her.

You cry and whimper when you hide her under the bedspread, the rug, or other places.

Are you nervous? You stick out your tongue when you are nervous.

Maybe you need to sit in time-out and think about why you need to be organized.

15

"Uh–huh."

I cry too. I don't want to see you unhappy.

And it takes a lot of time to find her.

Do you want us to solve this problem? It will take a lot of practice. I will help you.

Oh, are you telling Little River what we are talking about?

"Uh–huh."

Let's get started!

Leave Peanuts on the bed when you leave the bedroom.

21

Leave Peanuts on the rug in front of the kitchen sink when you leave the kitchen.

Leave Peanuts on the bathroom rug when you leave the bathroom.

Leave her in the garage when you ride in the ATV.

27

Leave Peanuts in front of the doggy door when you go to the garden.

29

You deserve a red sucker: You have been such a good listener.

I love you: You are almost perfect!

You share Peanuts with Little River.

You share your food with Little River.

And most importantly, you hugged and comforted PaPa when he was so sick:

I know you are very tired and want to go to sleep!

Sweet dreams and—remember—
if PaPa were here, he would say,
"Paris is *not almost perfect—she is
perfect!*

ABOUT THE AUTHOR

Dogs have always been the highlight of Connie Pitts's life. Each one loved her *unconditionally* as she did them.

Her thirty years of teaching children gave her a special insight into the healthy interaction between children and dogs.

Children love to hear about animals and can be led to develop good behaviors through their examples.

When she discovered this method, she became very excited about using this tool to teach children in many other areas.

Her next book will be about teaching children *Safety through Paris.*